This story appeared in the January 1924 issue of *The Blue Book Magazine*.

THE PLYMOUTH EXPRESS AFFAIR

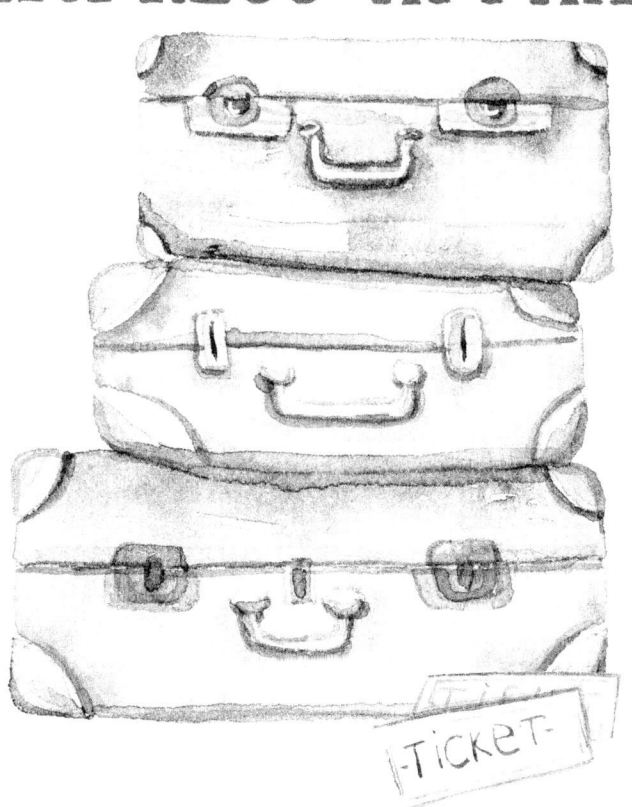

THE PLYMOUTH EXPRESS AFFAIR

A HERCULE POIROT SHORT STORY

AGATHA CHRISTIE

Isla Britannica Books

Isla Britannica Books is a Limited Company Registered in the United Kingdom. islabritannicabooks.com

Isla Britannica Books

First published in January 1924
2021 edition published by Isla Britannica Books in November 2021
Public domain copyright ©
Cover and new material copyright © Sarah Jane Weldon

Proud to be a member of the Alliance of Independent Authors. The moral right of the author and cover designer has been asserted. A CIP catalogue record is available from the British Library

All correspondence to Isla Britannica Books.

Join Sarah's community on Patreon: https://www.patreon.com/SarahJaneWeldon

This book follows **British English** spelling and usage.

DEDICATION

This edition of the book would not be possible without the love and support of my wonderful patrons and Kickstarter backers. Thank you to each and every one of you from the bottom of my heart.
Sarah (Founder of Isla Britannica Books) xx

KICKSTARTER BACKERS
- Jean Curran - Rose Sands - Madam Pince
- Dianne Ascroft - Maria Rosera - JJM93
- Jenny Burdinie - Bradley Walker - Kathy Robertson - Deana Potter
- Katy Ratcliffd - Herbie
- Nanciann Lamontagne - Sue Hampshire
- Valerie A Bedell - Gregory Tausch - Katie - Noelle
- Thatraja - Susan Schooler - Chaim S Weinberg
- Vikki - Lauren Ma - Aramanth Dawe - Treasa
- Nancy Pillot - Anne Newman - Polly Helms
- Linda H - Michelle Correll - SwordFirey
- Jerrie the filkferengi - Fiona L. Woods - Kristy C.

- Virginia Perkins Healy - K Collier - Tonia Williams - Jolie Castilla - Andrea Johnson - Dwayne Keller - RosieB - Lucy-Jean - Thyra

PATRONS
- Kristy C - Janice Paiano - Kathleen Fields - Tish Bouvier - Andrea Johnson - Gwendolyn Kielblock - Linda Hawkins - Amy Voros - Fiona L. Woods - Jean Curran - Jacquie Evans - Veronika Romero Getz - Virginia Perkins Healy - Mom-Mom Linda

THE PLYMOUTH EXPRESS AFFAIR
AGATHA CHRISTIE

Aboard the Plymouth Express train there is a strange smell of chloroform. It is soon found to come from a body under the seat - that of Mrs Rupert Carrington, pampered child of an American millionaire.

From *Poirot's Early Cases* and *The Under Dog and Other Stories*.

MEET THE CAST

Witnesses, Victims, and Suspects
Alec Simpson, R. N - passenger on the train, young naval officer
Captain Arthur J. M. Hastings, OBE - Poirot's companion-chronicler and best friend
Count de la Rochefour - mutual acquaintance and sender of a letter
Doctor - train passenger
Grace Kidd - jewel thief
Hercule Poirot - Belgian detective
Honorable Mrs. Rupert Carrington (Flossie) - deceased
Inspector Japp - Scotland Yard employee
Jane Mason - the maid
Mr. Ebenezer Halliday - father of the deceased
Mr Rupert Carrington - Flossie's husband
Paper-boy - newspaper and magazine seller
Red Narky - jewel thief

THE PLYMOUTH EXPRESS AFFAIR - A HERCULE POIROT SHORT STORY

Alec Simpson, R. N., stepped from the platform at Newton Abbot into a first-class compartment of the Plymouth Express. A porter followed him with a heavy suitcase. He was about to swing it up to the rack, but the young sailor stopped him.

"No—leave it on the seat. I'll put it up later. Here you are."

"Thank you, sir." The porter, generously tipped, withdrew.

Doors banged; a stentorian voice shouted: "Plymouth only. Change for Torquay. Plymouth next stop." Then a whistle blew, and the train drew slowly out of the station.

Lieutenant Simpson had the carriage to himself. The December air was chilly, and he pulled up the window. Then he sniffed vaguely, and frowned. What a smell there was! Reminded him of that time in hospital, and the operation on his leg. Yes, chloroform; that was it!

He let the window down again, changing his seat to one with its back to the engine. He pulled a pipe out of his pocket and lit it. For a little time he sat inactive, looking out into the night and smoking.

At last he roused himself, and opening the suitcase, took out some papers and magazines, then closed the suitcase again and endeavoured to shove it under the opposite seat—without success. Some hidden obstacle resisted it. He shoved harder with rising impatience, but it still stuck out halfway into the carriage.

"Why the devil wont it go in?" he muttered, and hauling it out completely, he stooped down and peered under the seat....

A moment later a cry rang out into the night, and the great train came to an unwilling halt in obedience to the imperative jerking of the communication-cord.

THE PLYMOUTH EXPRESS AFFAIR - A HERCULE POIROT SHORT STORY

"Mon ami," said Poirot. "You have, I know, been deeply interested in this mystery of the Plymouth Express. Read this."

I picked up the note he flicked across the table to me. It was brief and to the point.

Dear Sir:
I shall be obliged if you will call upon me at your earliest convenience.
Yours faithfully,
Ebenezer Halliday.

The connection was not clear to my mind, and I looked inquiringly at Poirot. For answer he took up the newspaper and read aloud:

"'A sensational discovery was made last night. A young naval officer returning to Plymouth found under the seat of his compartment, the body of a woman, stabbed through the heart. The officer at once pulled the communication-cord, and the train was brought to a standstill. The woman who was about thirty years of age, and richly dressed, has not yet been identified.'

"And later we have this: 'The woman found dead in the Plymouth Express has been identified as the Honorable Mrs. Rupert Carrington.' You see now, my friend? Or if you do not, I will add this. Mrs. Rupert Carrington was, before her marriage, Flossie Halliday, daughter of old man Halliday, the steel king of America."

"And he has sent for you? Splendid!"

"I did him a little service in the past—an affair of bearer bonds. And once, when I was in Paris for a royal visit, I had Mademoiselle Flossie pointed out to me. *La jolie petite pensionnaire!* She had the *jolie dot* too! It caused trouble. She nearly made a bad affair."

"How was that?"

"A certain Count de la Rochefour. *Un bien mauvais sujet!* A bad hat, as you would say. An adventurer pure and simple, who knew how to appeal to a romantic young girl. Luckily her father got wind of it in time. He took her back to America in haste. I heard of her marriage some years later, but I know nothing of her husband."

"H'm," I said. "The Honorable Rupert Carrington is no beauty, by all accounts. He'd pretty well run through his own money on the turf, and I should imagine old man Halliday's dollars came along in the nick of time. I should say that for a good-looking, well-mannered, utterly unscrupulous young scoundrel, it would be hard to find his match!"

"Ah, the poor little lady! *Elle n'est pas bien tombée!*"

"I fancy he made it pretty obvious at once that it was her money, and not she, that had attracted him. I believe they drifted apart almost at once. I have heard rumors lately that there was to be a definite legal separation."

"Old man Halliday is no fool. He would tie up her money pretty tight."

"I dare say. Anyway, I know as a fact that the Honorable Rupert is said to be extremely hard up."

"Ah-ha! I wonder—"

"You wonder what?"

"My good friend, do not jump down my throat like that. You are interested, I see. Supposing you accompany me to see Mr. Halliday. There is a taxi stand at the corner."

A very few minutes sufficed to whirl us to the superb house in Park Lane rented by the American magnate. We were shown into the library, and almost immediately we were joined by a large, stout man, with piercing eyes and an aggressive chin.

"M. Poirot?" said Mr. Halliday. "I guess I don't need to tell you what I want you for. You've read the papers, and I'm never one to let the grass grow under my feet. I happened to hear you were in London, and I remembered the good work you did over those bonds. Never forget a name. I've got the pick of Scotland Yard, but I'll have my own man as well. Money no object. All the dollars were made for my little girl—and now she's gone, I'll spend my last cent to catch the damned scoundrel that did it! See? So it's up to you to deliver the goods."

Poirot bowed.

"I accept, monsieur, all the more willingly that I saw your daughter in Paris several times. And now I will ask you to tell me the circumstances of her journey to Plymouth and any other details that seem to you to bear upon the case."

"Well, to begin with," responded Halliday, "she wasn't going to Plymouth. She was going to join a house-party at Avonmead Court, the Duchess of Swansea's place. She left

London by the twelve-fourteen from Paddington, arriving at Bristol (where she had to change) at two-fifty. The principal Plymouth expresses, of course, run via Westbury, and do not go near Bristol at all. The twelve-fourteen does a nonstop run to Bristol, afterward stopping at Weston, Taunton, Exeter and Newton Abbot. My daughter traveled alone in her carriage, which was reserved as far as Bristol, her maid being in a third-class carriage in the next coach."

Poirot nodded, and Mr. Halliday went on: "The party at Avonmead Court was to be a very gay one, with several balls, and in consequence my daughter had with her nearly all her jewels—amounting in value perhaps, to about a hundred thousand dollars."

"*Un moment*," interrupted Poirot. "Who had charge of the jewels? Your daughter, or the maid?"

"My daughter always took charge of them herself, carrying them in a small blue morocco case."

"Continue, monsieur."

"At Bristol the maid, Jane Mason, collected her mistress' dressing-bag and wraps, which were with her, and came to the door of Flossie's compartment. To her intense surprise, my daughter told her that she was not getting out at Bristol, but was going on farther. She directed Mason to get out the luggage and put it in the cloak-room. She could have tea in the refreshment-room, but she was to wait at the station for her mistress, who would return to Bristol by an up-train in the course of the afternoon. The maid, although very much astonished, did as she was told. She put the luggage in the cloak-room and had some tea. But up-train after up-train came in, and her mistress did not appear. After the arrival of the last train, she left the luggage where it was, and went to a hotel near the station for the night. This morning she read of the tragedy, and returned to town by the first available train."

"Is there nothing to account for your daughter's sudden change of plan?"

"Well, there is this: According to Jane Mason, at Bristol, Flossie was no longer alone in her carriage. There was a man in it who stood looking out of the farther window so that she could not see his face."

"The train was a corridor one, of course?"

"Yes."

"Which side was the corridor?"

"On the platform side. My daughter was standing in the corridor as she talked to Mason."

"And there is no doubt in your mind—excuse me!" He got up, and carefully straightened the inkstand which was a little askew. "*Je vous demande pardon*," he continued, reseating himself. "It affects my nerves to see anything crooked. Strange, is it not? I was saying, monsieur, that there is no doubt in your mind, as to this probably unexpected meeting being the cause of your daughter's sudden change of plan?"

"It seems the only reasonable supposition."

"You have no idea as to who the gentleman in question might be?"

The millionaire hesitated for a moment, and then replied.

"No—I do not know at all."

"Now—as to the discovery of the body?"

"It was discovered by a young naval officer who at once gave the alarm. There was a doctor on the train. He examined the body. She had been first chloroformed, and then stabbed. He gave it as his opinion that she had been dead about four hours, so it must have been done not long after leaving Bristol. —Probably between there and Weston, possibly between Weston and Taunton."

"And the jewel-case."

"The jewel-case, M. Poirot, was missing."

"One thing more, monsieur. Your daughter's fortune—to whom does it pass at her death?"

"Flossie made a will soon after her marriage, leaving everything to her husband." He hesitated for a minute, and then went on: "I may as well tell you, Monsieur Poirot, that I regard my son-in-law as an unprincipled scoundrel, and that, by my advice, my daughter was on the eve of freeing herself from him by legal means—no difficult matter. I settled her money upon her in such a way that he could not touch it during her lifetime, but although they have lived entirely apart for some years, she has frequently acceded to his demands for money, rather than face an open scandal. However, I was determined to put an end to this, and at last Flossie agreed, and my lawyers were instructed to take proceedings."

"And where is Monsieur Carrington?"

"In town. I believe he was away in the country yesterday, but he returned last night."

Poirot considered a little while. Then he said: "I think that is all, monsieur."

"You would like to see the maid, Jane Mason?"

"If you please."

Halliday rang the bell, and gave a short order to the footman. A few minutes later Jane Mason entered the room, a respectable, hard-featured woman, as emotionless in the face of tragedy as only a good servant can be.

"You will permit me to put a few questions? Your mistress, she was quite as usual before starting yesterday morning? Not excited or flurried?"

"Oh, no sir!"

"But at Bristol she was quite different?"

"Yes sir, regular upset—so nervous she didn't seem to know what she was saying."

"What did she say exactly?"

"Well sir, as near as I can remember, she said: 'Mason, I've got to alter my plans. Something has happened—I mean, I'm not getting out here after all. I must go on. Get out the luggage and put it in the cloak-room; then have some tea, and wait for me in the station.'

"'Wait for you here, ma'am?' I asked.

"'Yes, yes. Don't leave the station. I shall return by a later train. I don't know when. It mayn't be until quite late.'

"'Very well, ma'am,' I says. It wasn't my place to ask questions, but I thought it very strange."

"It was unlike your mistress, eh?"

"Very unlike her, sir."

"What did you think?"

"Well sir, I thought it was to do with the gentleman in the carriage. She didn't speak to him, but she turned round once or twice as though to ask him if she was doing right."

"But you didn't see the gentleman's face?"

"No sir; he stood with his back to me all the time."

"Can you describe him at all?"

"He had on a light fawn overcoat, and a traveling cap.

He was tall and slender, like, and the back of his head was dark."

"You didn't know him?"

"Oh, no, I don't think so, sir."

"It was not your master, Mr. Carrington, by any chance?"

Mason looked rather startled.

"Oh! I don't think so, sir!"

"But you are not *sure?*"

"It was about the master's build, sir—but I never thought of it being him. We so seldom saw him. I couldn't say it *wasn't* him!"

Poirot picked up a pin from the carpet, and frowned at it severely; then he continued: "Would it be possible for the man to have entered the train at Bristol before you reached the carriage?"

Mason considered.

"Yes sir, I think it would. My compartment was very crowded, and it was some minutes before I could get out—and then there was a very large crowd on the platform, and that delayed me too. But he'd only have had a minute or two to speak to the mistress, that way. I took it for granted that he'd come along the corridor."

"That is more probable, certainly."

He paused, still frowning.

"You know how the mistress was dressed, sir?"

"The papers give a few details, but I would like you to confirm them."

"She was wearing a white fox fur toque, sir, with a white spotted veil, and a blue frieze coat and skirt—the shade of blue they call electric."

"H'm, rather striking."

"Yes," remarked Halliday. "Inspector Japp is in hopes

that that may help us to fix the spot where the crime took place. Anyone who saw her would remember her."

"*Précisément!* —Thank you, mademoiselle." The maid left the room.

"Well!" Poirot got up briskly. "That is all I can do here —except, monsieur, that I would ask you to tell me everything—but *everything*!"

"I have done so."

"You are sure?"

"Absolutely."

"Then there is nothing more to be said. I must decline the case."

"Why?"

"Because you have not been frank with me."

"I assure you—"

"No, you are keeping something back."

There was a moment's pause, and then Halliday drew a paper from his pocket and handed it to my friend.

"I guess that's what you're after, Monsieur Poirot— though how you know about it fairly gets my goat!"

Poirot smiled, and unfolded the paper. It was a letter written in thin sloping handwriting. Poirot read it aloud.

"'Chère Madame:

"'It is with infinite pleasure that I look forward to the felicity of meeting you again. After your so amiable reply to my letter, I can hardly restrain my impatience. I have never forgotten those days in Paris. It is most cruel that you should be leaving London tomorrow. However, before very long, and perhaps sooner than you think, I shall have the joy of beholding once more the lady whose image has ever reigned supreme in my heart.

"'Believe, chère madame, all the assurances of my most devoted and unaltered sentiments—

"'Armand de la Rochefour.'"

Poirot handed the letter back to Halliday with a bow.

"I fancy, monsieur, that you did not know that your daughter intended renewing her acquaintance with the Count de la Rochefour?"

"It came as a thunderbolt to me! I found this letter in my daughter's handbag. As you probably know, Monsieur Poirot, this so-called count is an adventurer of the worst type."

Poirot nodded.

"But what I want to know is how you knew of the existence of this letter?"

My friend smiled. "Monsieur, I did not. But to track footmarks, and recognize cigarette-ash is not sufficient for a detective. He must also be a good psychologist! I knew that you disliked and mistrusted your son-in-law. He benefits by your daughter's death; the maid's description of the mysterious man bears a sufficient resemblance to him. Yet you are not keen on his track! Why? Surely because your suspicions lie in another direction. Therefore you were keeping something back."

"You're right, Monsieur Poirot. I was sure of Rupert's guilt until I found this letter. It unsettled me horribly."

"Yes. The Count says: 'Before very long, and perhaps sooner than you think.' Obviously he would not want to wait until you should get wind of his reappearance. Was it he who traveled down from London by the twelve-fourteen, and came along the corridor to your daughter's compartment? The Count de la Rochefour is also, if I remember rightly, tall and dark!"

The millionaire nodded.

"Well, monsieur, I will wish you good day. Scotland Yard, has, I presume, a list of the jewels?"

"Yes, I believe Inspector Japp is here now if you would like to see him."

THE PLYMOUTH EXPRESS AFFAIR

Japp was an old friend of ours, and greeted Poirot with a sort of affectionate contempt.

"And how are you, monsieur? No bad feeling between us, though we *have* got our different ways of looking at things. How are the 'little gray cells,' eh? Going strong?"

Poirot beamed upon him. "They function, my good Japp; assuredly they do!"

"Then that's all right. Think it was the Honorable Rupert, or a crook? We're keeping an eye on all the regular places, of course. We shall know if the shiners are disposed of, and of course whoever did it isn't going to keep them to admire their sparkle. Not likely! I'm trying to find out where Rupert Carrington was yesterday. Seems a bit of a mystery about it. I've got a man watching him."

"A great precaution, but perhaps a day late," suggested Poirot gently.

"You always will have your joke, Monsieur Poirot. Well, I'm off to Paddington. Bristol, Weston, Taunton, that's my beat. So long."

"You will come round and see me this evening, and tell me the result?"

"Sure thing, if I'm back."

"That good Inspector believes in matter in motion," murmured Poirot as our friend departed. "He travels; he measures footprints; he collects mud and cigarette-ash! He is extremely busy! He is zealous beyond words! And if I mentioned psychology to him, do you know what he would do, my friend? He would smile! He would say to himself: 'Poor old Poirot! He ages! He grows senile!' Japp is the 'younger generation knocking on the door.' And *ma foi!* They are so busy knocking that they do not notice that the door is open!"

"And what are you going to do?"

"As we have *carte blanche*, I shall expend threepence in ringing up the Ritz—where you may have noticed our Count is staying. After that, as my feet are a little damp, and I have sneezed twice, I shall return to my rooms and make myself a *tisano* over the spirit lamp!"

I did not see Poirot again until the following morning. I found him placidly finishing his breakfast.

"Well?" I inquired eagerly. "What has happened?"

"Nothing."

"But Japp?"

"I have not seen him."

"The Count?"

"He left the Ritz the day before yesterday."

"The day of the murder?"

"Yes."

"Then that settles it! Rupert Carrington is cleared."

"Because the Count de la Rochefour has left the Ritz? You go too fast, my friend."

"Anyway, he must be followed, arrested! But what could be his motive?"

"One hundred thousand dollars' worth of jewellery is a very good motive for anyone. No, the question to my mind is: why kill her? Why not simply steal the jewels? She would not prosecute."

"Why not?"

"Because she is a woman, *mon ami*. She once loved this man. Therefore she would suffer her loss in silence. And the Count, who is an extremely good psychologist where women are concerned,—hence his successes,—would know that perfectly well! On the other hand, if Rupert Carrington killed her, why take the jewels, which would incriminate him fatally?"

"As a blind."

"Perhaps you are right, my friend. Ah, here is Japp! I recognise his knock."

The Inspector was beaming good-humouredly.

"Morning, Poirot. Only just got back. I've done some good work! And you?"

THE PLYMOUTH EXPRESS AFFAIR

"Me, I have arranged my ideas," replied Poirot placidly.

Japp laughed heartily.

"Old chap's getting on in years," he observed beneath his breath to me. "That wont do for us young folk," he said aloud.

"*Quel dommage?*" Poirot inquired.

"Well, do you want to hear what I've done?"

"You permit me to make a guess? You have found the knife with which the crime was committed by the side of the line between Weston and Taunton, and you have interviewed the paper-boy who spoke to Mrs. Carrington at Weston!"

Japp's jaw fell. "How on earth did you know? Don't tell me it was those almighty 'little grey cells' of yours!"

"I am glad you admit for once that they are *all mighty*! Tell me, did she give the paper-boy a shilling for himself?"

"No, it was half a crown!" Japp recovered his temper and grinned. "Pretty extravagant, these rich Americans!"

"And in consequence the boy did not forget her?"

"Not he. Half-crowns don't come his way every day. She hailed him and bought two magazines. One had a picture of a girl in blue on the cover. 'That'll match me,' she said. Oh! he remembered her perfectly. Well, that was enough for me. By the doctor's evidence, the crime *must* have been committed before Taunton. I guessed they'd throw the knife away at once, and I walked down the line looking for it; and sure enough, there it was. I made inquiries at Taunton about our man, but of course it's a big station, and it wasn't likely they'd notice him. He probably got back to London by a later train."

Poirot nodded. "Very likely."

"But I found another bit of news when I got back. They're passing the jewels, all right! That large emerald was pawned last night—by one of the regular lot. Who do you think it was?"

"I don't know—except that he was a short man."

Japp stared. "Well, you're right there. He's short enough. It was Red Narky."

"Who on earth is Red Narky?" I asked.

"A particularly sharp jewel-thief, sir. And not one to stick at murder. Usually works with a woman—Gracie Kidd; but she doesn't seem to be in it this time—unless she's got off to Holland with the rest of the swag."

"You've arrested Narky?"

"Sure thing. But mind you, it's the other man we want—the man who went down with Mrs. Carrington in the train. He was the one who planned the job, right enough. But Narky wont squeal on a pal."

I noticed that Poirot's eyes had become very green.

"I think," he said gently, "that I can find Narky's pal for you, all right."

"One of your little ideas, eh?" Japp eyed Poirot sharply. "Wonderful how you manage to deliver the goods sometimes, at your age and all. Devil's own luck, of course."

"Perhaps, perhaps," murmured my friend. "Hastings, my hat. And the brush. So! My galoshes if it still rains! We must not undo the good work of that *tisano*. Au revoir, Japp!"

"Good luck to you, Poirot."

Poirot hailed the first taxi we met, and directed the driver to Park Lane.

When we drew up before Halliday's house, he skipped out nimbly, paid the driver and rang the bell. To the footman who opened the door he made a request in a low voice, and we were immediately taken upstairs. We went up to the top of the house, and were shown into a small neat bedroom.

Poirot's eyes roved round the room and fastened themselves on a small black trunk. He knelt in front of it, scrutinised the labels on it, and took a small twist of wire from his pocket.

"Ask Mr. Halliday if he will be so kind as to mount to me here," he said over his shoulder to the footman.

> *(It is suggested that the reader pause in his perusal of the story at this point, make his own solution of the mystery—and then see how close he comes to that of the author.—The Editors.)*

The man departed, and Poirot gently coaxed the lock of the trunk with a practiced hand. In a few minutes the lock gave, and he raised the lid of the trunk. Swiftly he began rummaging among the clothes it contained, flinging them out on the floor.

There was a heavy step on the stairs, and Halliday entered the room.

"What in hell are you doing here?" he demanded, staring.

"I was looking, monsieur, for *this*." Poirot withdrew from the trunk a coat and skirt of bright blue frieze, and a small toque of white fox fur.

"What are you doing with my trunk?" I turned to see that the maid, Jane Mason, had just entered the room.

"If you will just shut the door, Hastings. Thank you.

Yes, and stand with your back against it. Now, Mr. Halliday, let me introduce you to Grace Kidd, otherwise Jane Mason, who will shortly rejoin her accomplice, Red Narky, under the kind escort of Japp."

"It was of the most simple." Poirot waved a deprecating hand, then helped himself to more caviare. It is not every day that one lunches with a millionaire.

"It was the maid's insistence on the clothes that her mistress was wearing that first struck me. Why was she so anxious that our attention should be directed to them? I reflected that we had only the maid's word for the mysterious man in the carriage at Bristol. As far as the doctor's evidence went, Mrs. Carrington might easily have been murdered *before* reaching Bristol. But if so, then the maid must be an accomplice. And if she were an accomplice, she would not wish this point to rest on her evidence alone. The clothes Mrs. Carrington was wearing were of a striking nature. A maid usually has a good deal of choice as to what her mistress shall wear. Now if, after Bristol, anyone saw a lady in a bright blue coat and skirt, and a fur toque, he will be quite ready to swear he has seen Mrs. Carrington.

"I began to reconstruct. The maid would provide herself with duplicate clothes. She and her accomplice chloroform and stab Mrs. Carrington between London and Bristol, probably taking advantage of a tunnel. Her body is rolled under the seat; the maid takes her place. At Weston she must make herself noticed. How? In all probability, a newspaper-boy will be selected. She will insure his remembering her by giving him a large tip. She also drew his attention to the colour of her dress by a remark about one of the magazines. After leaving Weston, she throws the knife out of the window to mark the place where the crime presumably occurred, and changes her clothes, or buttons a long mackintosh over them. At Taunton she leaves the train and returns to Bristol as soon as possible, where her accomplice has duly left the luggage in the cloak-room. He hands over the ticket and himself returns to London. She waits on the platform, carrying out her role, goes to a hotel for the night and returns to town in the morning exactly as she said.

"When Japp returned from his expedition, he confirmed all my deductions. He also told me that a well-known crook was passing the jewels. I knew that whoever it was would be the exact opposite of the man Jane Mason described. When I heard that it was Red Narky, who always worked with Gracie Kidd—well, I knew just where to find her."

"And the Count?"

"The more I thought of it, the more I was convinced that he had nothing to do with it. That gentleman is much too careful of his own skin to risk murder. It would be out of keeping with his character."

"Well, Monsieur Poirot," said Halliday. "I owe you a big debt. And the cheque I write after lunch wont go near to settling it."

Poirot smiled modestly, and murmured to me: "The good Japp, he shall get the official credit, all right, but though he has got his Gracie Kidd, I think that I, as the Americans say, have got his goat!"

FINIS

Find Your Next Book Here

Become a patron for £1 a month and get my next book and audiobook for free, before anyone else, and your name on the dedication page of future books.
https://www.patreon.com/SarahJaneWeldon

GLOSSARY

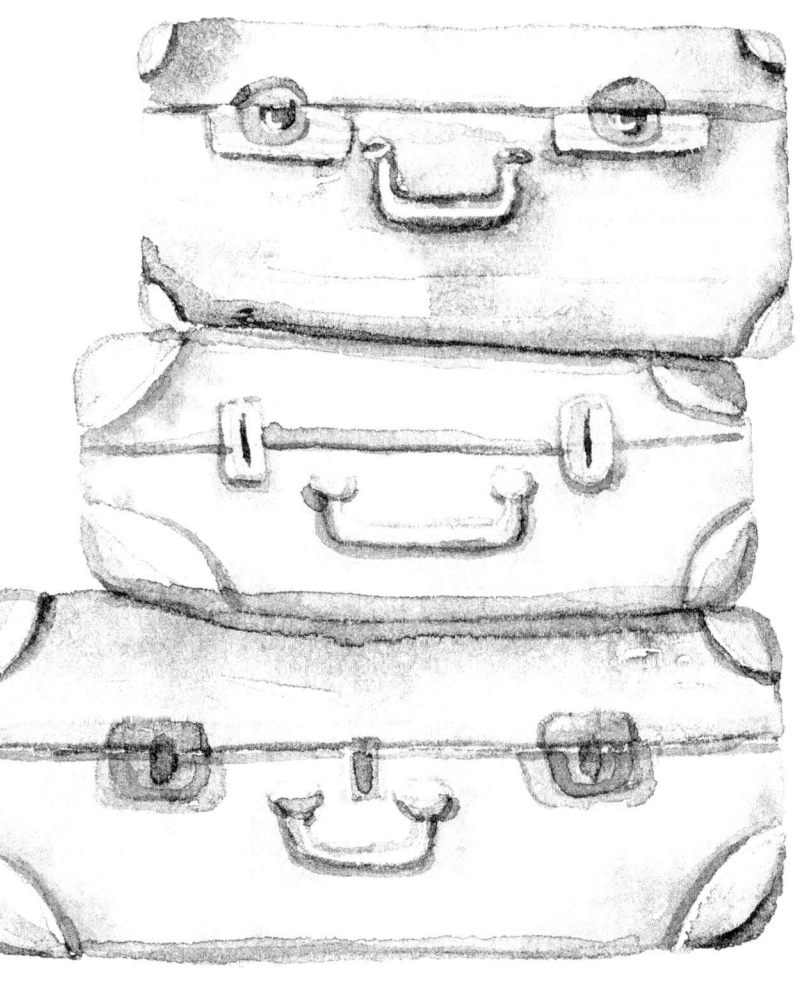

GLOSSARY

Frieze: a type of decoration, long and thin, often a painting or sculpture
Galoshes: waterproof overshoes, often made of rubber got his goat. A bit like ankle height wellies
Mackintosh: a waterproof outercoat or rain coat, very British, sometimes shortened to 'mac' (better put my mac on, looks like rain)
Stentorian: a voice that is loud and powerful
Tisano: a herbal chocolate tea

Have you Read…

THE GREAT BRITISH STAKE OFF

A VAMPIRE COZY MYSTERY, MOVIE SET MURDERS

Sarah Jane Weldo[n]

ACKNOWLEDGEMENT

Very special thanks to my lovely patrons, without whom I wouldn't be writing or publishing these books at all.

Copyright © Sarah Jane Weldon 2021
All rights reserved.
www.sarahweldon.co.uk

This book is a work of fiction. Names, characters, businesses, places, events, locales, and incidents are either the products of the author's imagination or used in a fictitious manner. Any resemblance to actual persons, living or dead, or actual events is purely coincidental.

No part of this publication (with the exception of public domain works) may be reproduced, distributed, or transmitted in any form or by any means, including photocopying, recording, or other electronic or mechanical methods, without the prior written permission of the publisher, except in the case of brief quotations embodied in critical reviews and certain other noncommercial uses permitted by copyright law. For permission requests, write to the publisher, addressed "Attention: Permissions Coordinator," at the address below.

Isla Britannica Books
C/O Waltons Clark Whitehill
Chartered Accountants & Business Advisers

Maritime House
Harbour Walk
The Marina
Hartlepool TS24 0UX

Patreon
Become a patron for £1 a month and get my next book and audiobook for free, before anyone else, and your name on the dedication page of future books.
https://www.patreon.com/SarahJaneWeldon

Cozy Mystery Book Explorer Facebook Group
Share your favourite cozy mystery books, movies, and tv series with other fans of the genre.
https://www.facebook.com/groups/1072107036292229/

ALSO BY ISLA BRITANNICA BOOKS

Coffee Shop Mystery Series

Dead on Doughnuts

Extra Shots

Cupcaked Crime

Cozy Collie Mystery Series

Baa'd to the Bone

Talk is Sheep

Silence of the Lambs

Movie Set Murders Series

The Great British Stake Off

The Antiques Ghost Show

Fright Night at the Movies

Christmas Standalone Series

Ding Dong Merrily and Die

The Last Christmas

Let it Dough, Let it Dough, Let it Dough

British Seaside Mystery Series

Murder in the Rigging

Murder at the Lido

Fry Another Day

A Game of Cones

The Poison in the Soup

Funeral Parlour Mystery Series

A Grave Mistake

STEAM PUNK MYSTERY SERIES

Your Mummy or Your Life

Pain in the Asp

AIRPORT MYSTERY SERIES

Flight to the Death

Final Destination

Eternal Departure

GRIME FIGHTER MYSTERY SERIES

Poisoned in Paradise

Peril in Paradise

Panic in Paradise

ALICE IN WONDERLAND MYSTERY SERIES

On Burrowed Time

THE WRONG AGATHA MYSTERY SERIES

What Would Agatha Do?

What Agatha Did

What Agatha Did Next

DEATH IS VINYL SERIES

Suspicious Sleeves

The Vinyl Countdown

Record Slayer

MURDER IN THE '50S MYSTERY SERIES

Pink Heels and Problems

Red Heels and Renegades

Black Heels and Bloodshed

KNITTY CAT MYSTERY SERIES

Knit One, Purrl Two

A Tight Knit Alibi

Knot Your Average Cat

BEAGLE MYSTERY SERIES

Where Beagles Dare

Beagle Eyed and Dangerous

Spread Beagled

FOOD BLOGGER MYSTERY SERIES

One Slice of Murder

House Salad Suspects

Well Done and Deadly

HAIR RAISING MYSTERY SERIES

A Brush with Death

Curl Up and Fry

Comb Out and Mangle

MURDER AT THE NORTH POLE MYSTERY SERIES

Deerly Departed

Hold on for Deer Life

The Final sleigh. Oh, Deer!

GUY FAV'KES NIGHT STANDALONE SERIES

Expecto Petroleum

MURDER ONCE AND FLORAL MYSTERY SERIES

Of Tulips and Trouble

Of Daffodils and Death

Of Crocuses and Confessions

DEAD BEFORE BREAKFAST MYSTERY SERIES

Poison in the Pancakes

Waffle Wrong Doings

Murder Over Easy

TWELVE DEADLY DAYS OF CHRISTMAS MYSTERY SERIES

A Partridge in a Pear Tree

Two Turtle Doves

Three French Hens

Four Calling Birds

Five Gold Rings

Six Geese A-Laying

Seven Swans A-Swimming

Eight Maids A-Milking

Nine Ladies Dancing

Ten Lords A-Leaping

Eleven Pipers Piping

Twelve Drummers Drumming

BREW TO A KILL MYSTERY SERIES

Rose Tea and Revenge

Malva Tea and Murder

Vanilla Tea and Violence

DIGS, DEATH, AND DENIAL MYSTERY SERIES

Hearse of the Pharaohs

Stalk Like an Egyptian

Tomb with a View

LADY ADELAIDE VICTORIAN MYSTERY SERIES

These Boots are Made for Corpsing

Dead Soles Can't Talk

A Bootiful Day to Die

NAIL SALON MYSTERY SERIES

The Weakest Pink

Caught Red Handed

Death of a Nails Man

MURDER DOWN UNDER MYSTERY SERIES

Koalified to Murder

Emulated Murder

Kangarooting for Murder

SILENT BUNDT DEADLY MYSTERY SERIES

Gone Bundt Not Forgotten

Nothing Bundt Skin and Bones

Last Bundt Not Least

IT'S A VINE LIFE MYSTERY SERIES

A Pour Decision

A Blush with Death

In the Dead of Vintner

ESTATE AGENT TO THE DEAD MYSTERY SERIES

Booing Recommended

SHORT STORIES

The Astronaut

Morning Has Broken

Printed in Great Britain
by Amazon